6.8

5.

DATE DUE

THE AMAZON

written and photographed by

Julia Waterlow

RSVP
**RAINTREE
STECK-VAUGHN**
P U B L I S H E R S
The Steck-Vaughn Company

Austin, Texas

Cover: *Houses on riverbank of Amazon River*

Series and book editor: Rosemary Ashley
Designer: Derek Lee
Cover design: Scott Melcer

Library of Congress Cataloging-in-Publishing Data

Waterlow, Julia
    The Amazon / written and photographed by Julia Waterlow.
      p.   cm. — (Rivers of the world)
    Includes index.
    Summary: An overview of the Amazon River, its physical features, plants and wildlife, history, economics, towns and cities, vanishing Indians, and environmental threats.
      ISBN 0–8114–3101-0
      1. Amazon River—Juvenile literature.   [1. Amazon River.]
    I. Title.   II. Series: Rivers of the world (Austin, Tex.)
    F2546.W28 1993   92 25446
    981′.1—dc20   CIP
                                                                 AC

Typeset by Multifacit Graphics, Keyport, NJ
Printed in Italy by G. Canale & C.S.p.A.,Turin
Bound in the United States by Lake Book, Melrose Park, IL
1 2 3 4 5 6 7 8 9 0 LB 99 98 97 96 95 94

RIVERS OF THE WORLD

The Amazon
The Ganges
The Mississippi
The Nile
The Rhine
The Thames

CONTENTS

1
The Vast Amazon

Plunging from the snowy peaks of the Andes mountains, and flowing through the steamy heat of endless tropical rain forests, the vast Amazon River coils lazily east across South America. It finally pours out into the Atlantic Ocean 3,900 miles from its source. Although not quite the longest river in the world (the Nile is 155 miles longer) the Amazon is by far the biggest. So much water flows through it that it could fill the huge 7,540-square-mile Lake Ontario in three hours.

But the Amazon is much more than just one river. Like veins in a leaf, hundreds of small streams join larger ones and keep swelling until they reach the Amazon itself. The whole area, called the Amazon basin, is more than ten times the size of France. It covers more than half the land of South America, including much of Brazil and parts of Peru, Venezuela, Colombia, Ecuador, and Bolivia.

Most towns and villages lie beside the big rivers, which carve highways through the forests of the Amazon basin. The dense trees make exploring the Amazon region difficult and large areas are still unknown. Stories of gold, lost cities, and strange and wondrous people, animals, and plants, have made it seem a mysterious place. But the building of roads is changing all this, as people reach deep into previously remote areas, and clear the forest for development.

The Amazon is a treasure-trove of animals and plants. More varieties are found there than anywhere else in the world. Because it is one of the last big natural plant and animal reserves on our planet, many people are worried that it might be lost forever. No one knows how the rain forests could be useful to us in the future or what would happen to the world if they were destroyed. The Amazon's future is one of the great issues facing the world today.

Here 1,242 miles from the ocean, the Amazon River is almost like an inland sea.

The Physical Features

The upper and middle courses

A tiny stream trickles through spongy grass high in the Andes mountains. Even though it is close to the equator, at a height of 17,225 feet, the air is freezing cold. Beginning just 125 miles from the Pacific Ocean, this is the source of the Amazon. The tumbling stream joins the Apurimac River, cutting a deep valley that flows north—Apurimac means "Great Speaker" the name the Amazon Indians use to describe the roar of the river.

Like all rivers while they are young, here in the mountains it flows fast, crashing over boulders and tearing at the rocks it passes. Much of the loose material, called sediment, that the river picks up will be carried thousands of miles toward the sea. A scientist once estimated that it would take 9,000 trains pulling 30 ten-ton trucks every day to carry the same amount of sediment as the waters of the Amazon carry with it. During its first 620 miles the river plunges furiously over rapids and through steep-sided gorges.

Once it leaves the Andes, the Amazon is already twice the width of the Rhine, the largest river in Europe. It still has nearly 3,280 miles to go before reaching the ocean but has only 985 feet to fall. The Amazon slows down to a crawl and starts to flow east across the huge plain toward the Atlantic Ocean. In places it widens to several miles appearing more like a giant inland sea than a river. Sometimes you cannot even see the far side because of its tremendous size.

This small stream is the source of the great Amazon River. High in the Andes mountains, snow covers the peaks and little grows on the slopes below except rough grass.

The Amazon's tributaries

Like all rivers, the Amazon gathers water from other streams as it flows to the sea. These streams are called a river's tributaries. The Amazon has more than a thousand major tributaries: ten of these are more than 620 miles in length.

Although the Amazon rises in the Andes mountains, not all its tributaries start there. Some rivers, like the Trombetas, rise in the Guyana Highlands to the north, and others, like the Tapajós, begin in the Brazilian Highlands far to the south. The Amazon has the largest river catchment area in the world; the whole area covers more than half the land of South America.

The Amazon has several name changes on its route to the sea. Near its source, high in the Andes, it is the Apurimac; then it becomes the Ene, the Tambo, the Ucayali, and then the Amazon. When it leaves Peru and enters Brazil, it becomes the Solimioes, but it becomes the Amazon again after it meets the Rio Negro.

The catchment area of the Amazon basin.

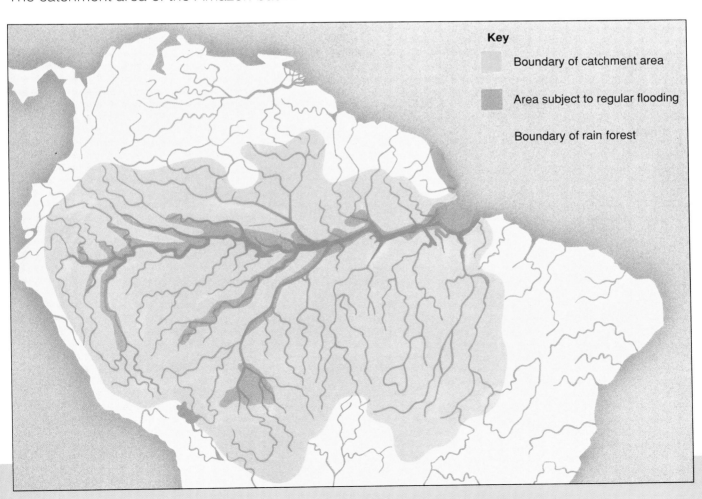

Key

Boundary of catchment area

Area subject to regular flooding

Boundary of rain forest

7

Here at Santarém, the clearwater Tapajós River meets the whitewater Amazon. For several miles the rivers run beside each other without mixing.

There are three different types of rivers in the Amazon basin. These are called whitewater, clearwater, and blackwater rivers. Whitewater rivers, like the Madeira, are actually a dirty yellow color. They are this shade because the water is full of sediment brought down from the soft rocks of the Andes mountains.

Clearwater rivers, like the Xingu, flow from the Brazilian Highlands. They are a blue-green color and carry little sediment in the water because the Highlands are made of hard rock which the river cannot easily erode.

There are also blackwater rivers which are the color of dark tea, such as the Rio Negro ("Rio" means river and "Negro" means black in Portuguese).

They too have little sediment. Sediment carries nutrients in it and so whitewater rivers have many more fish and other water creatures than the blackwater and clearwater rivers.

A storm sweeps across the sky. In some areas in the Amazon basin it rains nearly every day of the year.

8

Climate and water level

The size of a river is partly due to the distance it covers, because the farther it goes the more other rivers will feed it. But more important is the amount of rain that falls in the area. The Amazon basin is one of the wettest regions in the world, with an average of more than 100 inches of rain per year. Rainfall is highest near the Andes—there it can be over 236 inches per year. Although there is plenty of rain all year round, there are times when the rainfall is heavier than others. In these wet seasons the torrential rain swells the rivers. The river levels can change by up to 50 feet, twice the height of a two-story house. In many places the rivers overflow and there are floods. The floods can last from between four to seven months of the year.

The area which regularly floods is called the floodplain, known in the Amazon region as the *varzea*. When the river floods, it drops the sediment it has been carrying with it from the Andes. The rich nutrients in the sediment make the *varzea* one of the most fertile places in the entire area of the huge Amazon basin.

The *varzea* at the beginning of the wet season. Soon the cows will have to be moved to drier land.

Length: 3,900 miles
Average width: 1.2 to 3 miles
Number of tributaries: Over 10,000—the longest tributary is the Madeira River
Volume of water: 259,400 cu. yd. per second
Area of river basin: 2.3 million sq. miles
Deepest point: 121 feet, at Óbidos

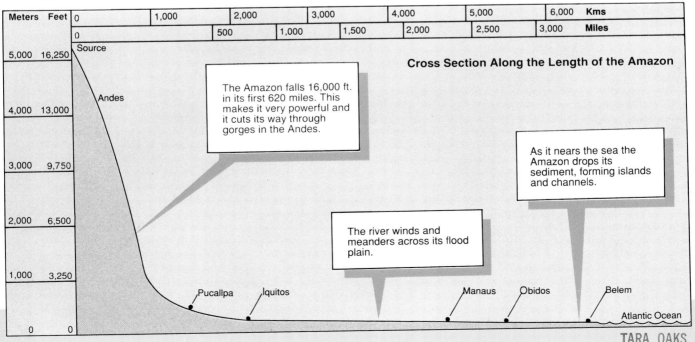

Cross Section Along the Length of the Amazon

The Amazon falls 16,000 ft. in its first 620 miles. This makes it very powerful and it cuts its way through gorges in the Andes.

As it nears the sea the Amazon drops its sediment, forming islands and channels.

The river winds and meanders across its flood plain.

9

This beach is near the mouth of the Tapajós River where it joins the Amazon. People from the town of Santarém come here to swim and picnic.

The lower course

As it nears the sea, the Amazon moves even more slowly and drops most of its huge load of sediment. It twists and turns through this mud and silt, forming thousands of islands which shift as sediment is added or washed away. There are channels between the islands, and it is difficult to tell which is the main river anymore.

The mouth of the Amazon is vast: its width stretches 205 miles across, about the same as the distance from London to Paris. The European explorers who first voyaged to the Amazon's mouth called it "Fresh Water Sea," because the river's flow is so powerful that it pushes fresh water out into the Atlantic Ocean for some 155 miles. In the middle of the river's mouth is Marajó, a huge island about the size of Switzerland.

The Amazon in prehistoric times

The Amazon has not always flowed into the Atlantic. Two hundred million years ago, South America and Africa were joined as part of one huge continent called Gondwanaland. At that time the Andes did not exist and the Amazon flowed west into the Pacific Ocean.

About 180 million years ago, the Earth's land masses began to break up. The continents of Africa and South America split apart, and the Andes mountains began to rise. The river could no longer flow into the Pacific Ocean and a huge lake formed, covering most of what is now the Amazon basin. Eventually the water found a way out, spilling over between the Brazilian and Guyana Highlands at Óbidos. The mighty Amazon River, as we know it, was formed.

3
Plants and Wildlife

In the bleak, windswept Andes it is difficult to imagine that tropical rain forests lie downstream. The cold and the wind make it hard for plants to grow in the high Andes mountains. There are just grasses and some stunted trees growing in sheltered places. But as the river drops down toward the plain and the temperature rises, more and more vegetation appears. On the edge of the Amazon basin there is so much rain that the mountains are covered in clouds and mists most of the time. Varieties of mosses and damp ferns cling to trees and rocky slopes.

The rain forest

Plants grow best where it is hot and wet. The equator runs through the middle of the Amazon basin so the region is always very warm. Add to this heavy rainfall all year round, and the result is thick tropical rain forest—one third of all that is left in the world. Most of the rain forest grows on dry land, called *terra firma* rain forest. The other main type is called *igapo*. This is forest near the rivers that is flooded during the wet season. The trees here do not grow as tall as in the *terra firma* forest.

Clouds and rain hang over the Amazon forest.

The roots of this tree are flooded during the wet season. This is *igapo* forest which is regularly covered by water.

In the past, people believed the Amazon rain forest was situated on fertile soil because plants grew so well. Now it has been found that this is not so; in fact most Amazon soils are very poor. Instead of nutrients from the soil, the *terra firma* forest depends on rain and rotting vegetation to provide the food needed. As plants die, they feed other plants. The shallow but thick roots hold the soil together and, like a sponge, they keep the nutrient-filled water from being washed out of the soil. Everything is recycled and in balance.

Animals and plants depend on each other too. Plants provide food for the animals, while the animals enrich the soil with their droppings. Animals also help to spread seeds, either in their droppings or by carrying them in their fur or feathers. If one type disappears, others could die out.

The trees of the rain forest are very important in the water cycle. A lot of the rain that falls is soaked up by the trees. Moisture is then given off from their leaves into the air. About half the Amazon's rainfall comes from water that has transpired from the trees.

A tropical forest has several layers. The top layer, the canopy, is the liveliest and noisiest place. In the crowded tops of the trees live animals like the leaf-eating sloth and many types of monkeys.

Birds such as parrots and toucans perch in the branches. Occasionally a giant tree with enormous roots, called an emergent, shoots up above the canopy. Most trees in the *terra firma* rain forest usually grow to between 80 and 100 feet, though emergents may be 200 feet high.

Below the canopy is the understory. There the rain forest is dark and gloomy, the tall tree trunks soar up like the columns in a cathedral. Hanging from the high branches like untidy ropes, or twisting around the trunks, are lianas and creepers. Some palms or ferns grow where light filters through, but otherwise little grows because there is not enough light. The forest floor is littered with rotting leaves and fallen branches. Lizards, beetles, ants, spiders, and other creatures make the forest floor home.

Rain forest plants

A group of plants called epiphytes grow in the rain forest. They grow on other plants, usually high up on trees so they can get light. There are many types of epiphytes in the Amazon basin—orchids are the most famous. They do not take food from the tree but produce their own by photosynthesis. There are also plants called bromeliads: their tough leaves form a cup in which water is stored. Bromeliads are members of the pine-apple family.

The rivers have their own plant life too. Huge Victoria Amazonica water lilies grow in lakes or on the flooded *varzea*. What looks like a grassy island floats down the river; it is made of matted grasses so thick that other plants, even small shrubs, can seed and grow

This diagram shows the different layers of the rain forest.

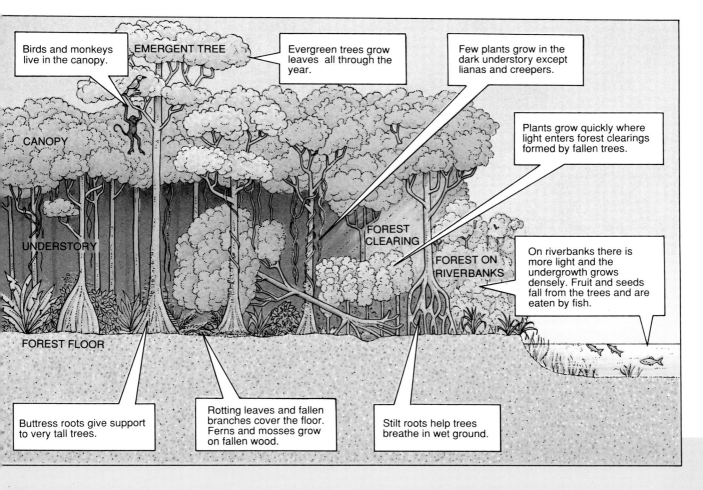

Birds and monkeys live in the canopy.

EMERGENT TREE

Evergreen trees grow leaves all through the year.

Few plants grow in the dark understory except lianas and creepers.

Plants grow quickly where light enters forest clearings formed by fallen trees.

CANOPY

FOREST CLEARING

FOREST ON RIVERBANKS

On riverbanks there is more light and the undergrowth grows densely. Fruit and seeds fall from the trees and are eaten by fish.

UNDERSTORY

FOREST FLOOR

Buttress roots give support to very tall trees.

Rotting leaves and fallen branches cover the floor. Ferns and mosses grow on fallen wood.

Stilt roots help trees breathe in wet ground.

13

there. Insects live in the floating greenery, and perched on top are often water birds, such as white egrets.

Nowhere else on Earth does such a wide variety of species of plants exist. No one knows for sure, but there are probably more than 50,000 different kinds. In two and a half acres, you can find about 200 varieties of trees, whereas in America there might be ten. Even though there are so many different types, there may only be a few of each in the whole Amazon basin. There are still thousands of species to be discovered.

Some of the Amazon's plants are used by humans; the Indians of the Amazon have known about their uses for hundreds of years, both for food and for medicine. Several Amazon plants have proved to be very important: today, 25 percent of our medicines come from rain forest plants. One example is curare, a poison used by the Indians, which is now the base for many drugs used for medical purposes. It is believed there may be plants, yet undiscovered, which could provide cures for diseases such as cancer and AIDS.

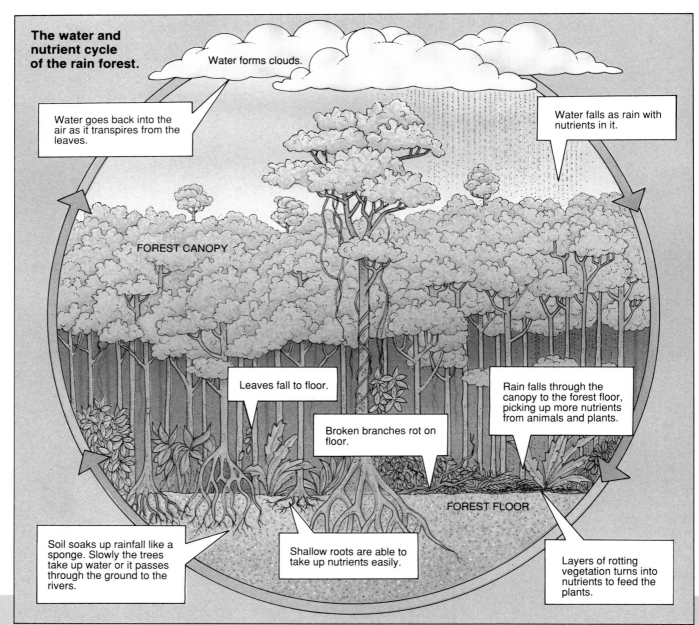

The water and nutrient cycle of the rain forest.

Water forms clouds.

Water goes back into the air as it transpires from the leaves.

Water falls as rain with nutrients in it.

FOREST CANOPY

Leaves fall to floor.

Broken branches rot on floor.

Rain falls through the canopy to the forest floor, picking up more nutrients from animals and plants.

FOREST FLOOR

Soil soaks up rainfall like a sponge. Slowly the trees take up water or it passes through the ground to the rivers.

Shallow roots are able to take up nutrients easily.

Layers of rotting vegetation turns into nutrients to feed the plants.

14

Products of the rain forest

Some hardwood trees, like rosewood and mahogany, are very valuable. So much rosewood has been cut down that it is now quite difficult to find. Although not all the trees are harvested (many of the Amazon hardwoods are too hard even to be cut) others provide fruit and nuts. Some of these, like Brazil nuts, are

Some giant Victoria Amazonica water lilies are more than three feet across. Underneath they are covered with thorns to protect them from plant-eating fish.

Big buttress roots stick out of either side at the base of the trunk to support the tallest Amazon trees, some of which reach a great height.

exported abroad, but many of the thousands of exotic and tasty fruits found there are never seen outside the Amazon basin. Fragrant oils from the Amazon's plants are becoming popular—like patchouli, rosewood, andiroba, and copaiba. Cacao seeds, which are used to make cocoa and chocolate, come originally from the rain forest. The white sap of trees like rubber and sorva (which is used in making chewing gum) are important forest products too.

Animal life

The wildlife in the Amazon is as varied as the plant life. Three thousand varieties of freshwater fish have been found, in addition to one fifth of all species of birds in the world, and millions of types of insects. These include the arawana, which leaps out of the water to grab insects and spiders off trees; the dangerous, meat-eating piranha fish; the huge piracuru, which has a tongue so hard

Forest products are sold on the streets of towns in the Amazon region. Products such as the bark or leaves of special trees are sold to be boiled in water and used as medicines.

16

A sloth hangs upside down high up in a tree, looking for tasty leaves to eat. It clings on to the branch with its claws. Sloths climb easily, although they are very slow. On the ground they can only crawl awkwardly and are almost defenseless.

that it can be used as a grater; and the electric eel, which can stun its victims with up to 500 volts of electricity.

There are gentle giants too, such as the manatee, a fish-like mammal believed to have evolved from the same ancestor as the elephant. The Amazon's

dolphins and stingrays are freshwater descendants of seawater creatures. As well as feeding off other fish and water plants, many of the Amazon fish also eat fruit and seeds which fall off trees into the water, particularly in the *igapo* forest when it floods.

Above Capybaras browse near a riverbank. They are the world's largest rodents.

The largest animals in the Amazon are the jaguar (a member of the cat family) and the long-nosed tapir (a relative of the rhinoceros). The anteater is never short of food because of the millions of ants that swarm all over the forest floor. By the water's edge lives the capybara. It is the largest rodent in the world, like a very large guinea pig, and it likes to swim in the shallow water. Other creatures, such as porcupines, scurry across the forest floor, and vampire bats fly among the trees. Swimming in the water might be an anaconda, the largest snake in the world, sometimes measuring up to 33 feet long. Basking in the sun on the riverbank are alligators and turtles, while colorful butterflies flutter around their heads.

Alligators bask in the sun beside a river. Many of them are killed for their valuable hides.

4
Explorers and Settlers

The first settlers

Native American peoples were living in the Amazon region long before Europeans came to South America. It is thought they originally came from Asia about ten thousand years ago, and spread south through the Americas. In the Andes, they created highly developed civilizations such as the Inca Empire, but the forest peoples lived much simpler lives in individual tribes. Little remains to give us clues about their history, but fine pottery dating back to about 1500 B.C. has been found on Marajó Island.

This nineteenth-century painting shows a wild, untamed world of water and dense vegetation.

The arrival of the Europeans

It was not until 1500 A.D. that Europeans came to the Amazon region. A Spanish sailor named Vicente Pinzón found fresh water far out in the Atlantic Ocean and traced it back to the mouth of the Amazon. From 1500 onward, Portuguese settlers arrived on the coast of Brazil, and Spaniards started their conquest of the Inca Empire in Peru. The Spanish had heard stories of El Dorado, the king of a land rich with gold, and believed his kingdom lay in the

Left and below Two engravings of the Amazon. One shows the huge mouth of the river. The other shows explorers dragging their boats around falls on the Madeira River, upstream from Porto Velho.

Churches like this were built on the banks of remote tributaries of the Amazon. European priests and missionaries converted many Indians to Christianity.

unexplored land east of the Andes.

The first Europeans to travel along the Amazon River were Spaniards led by an army officer named Francisco de Orellana. In 1541 he set out from Ecuador as part of a huge expedition to search for the fabled gold. The Spaniards took with them a number of native peoples of the Amazon region (whom they called Indians), together with llamas, dogs, horses, and pigs. Most of the native peoples and the animals soon died of starvation or disease in the tropical heat of the forests.

2

Christian missionaries traveled deep into the Amazon basin. Even today they still run schools for the local children.

Ten months into the trip, de Orellana was sent ahead with sixty men to travel downriver in search of food. They tried to row back upriver, and when they found they could not they decided to continue. They, too, nearly starved and were reduced to eating their leather belts and shoe soles. Many Amerindian tribes lived along the riverbanks; some helped the Spaniards and others attacked them. Among one tribe the men saw female warriors: they reminded the Spaniards of the war-like women in ancient Greek myths called Amazons—and so the river got its name. A year and a half later, de Orellana arrived at the mouth of the Amazon.

European settlers, mainly Portuguese, came to the Amazon basin in the late 1500s. The only way to travel through the forest was by river, so settlements were built on riverbanks. The settlers grew tobacco and sugarcane as well as food crops.

At this time, the only Europeans to venture deep into the forests were adventurers seeking gold and slaves, and Jesuit priests looking for native peoples whom they could convert to Christianity. Although some Europeans traded with native peoples and even married them, thousands were taken as slaves to work on sugarcane plantations near the coast. Many natives died.

Scientists and naturalists

In the eighteenth and nineteenth centuries the main explorers of the Amazon were scientists. They brought back to Europe fantastic stories of what they had seen. In 1743, Charles de La Condamine returned with the first real scientific information about the river, the plants, and the people. He was followed by Baron Alexander von Humboldt in 1800, who was the first person to test the electric eel. He gave himself shock after shock in his experiments to see which part of the eel was dangerous.

Many scientists from different countries plunged into the depths of the Amazon rain forest. Three of the best-known nineteenth-century figures were Alfred Wallace, Henry Bates, and Richard Spruce. They all spent many

Above A naturalist's drawing showing the buttress roots of a giant Amazon tree.

Left A drawing of Henry Bates being attacked by toucans in the rain forest.

years there, studying animals and plants. There were many dangers for them, particularly diseases like malaria, as well as poisonous plants and animals, and unfriendly tribes. Food was often difficult to find and there was no help when they were in trouble. Today, many scientists continue to study the Amazon region because of its plants and animals, found nowhere else in the world. Even though travel to the Amazon is a little easier and more accessible now, it is still a wild place to explore.

Industry, Trade, and Transportation

Exploiting the natural resources

The Europeans who came to the Amazon basin believed they would find untold riches that would make them fabulously wealthy. The first Portuguese found and exported brazilwood, which produces a red dye. They also took many of the native people away and forced them into slavery, but they found little else of use to them. Settlers who came to the Amazon region grew crops and traded tobacco and sugarcane. The dream of rich treasures did not come true until the nineteenth century. "Black gold" grew wild in the Amazon rain forest: this was rubber.

People already knew of a few uses for rubber, but it was Charles Goodyear's discovery in 1839 that changed the history of the Amazon. He found out how rubber could be made stronger and more elastic; and this in turn led to John Boyd Dunlop's invention of the rubber tire in 1888. The age of the motor car had begun and there was a great de-

This tiny factory produces rubber gloves from rubber grown in the area.

mand for rubber. The price for rubber soared all over the world. People streamed into the Amazon region, hoping to find it and make their fortunes.

Many were successful. For the next twenty-five years the towns along the Amazon river prospered. In Iquitos, Manaus, and Belém, elegant women wore the latest European fashions.

João, rubber tapper

"I am a *seringeiro,* which is what we call a rubber tapper in Brazil. I live by the Rio Madeira. I start every day by going round the rubber trees that grow wild in the forest. I make a small cut in the bark of each tree. Underneath the cut is a little cup, into which flows the white sap from the tree, called latex. I go round the trees later in the day to collect the latex. I can cut up to 80 trees a day. I don't make much money because the price of rubber is low."

This train is all that is left of a railway built to bring Bolivian rubber to Porto Velho during the rubber boom in the early twentieth century.

Alongside the existing small shacks appeared grand buildings of stone, and marble palaces. Because there is no stone in the heart of the Amazon basin, ships had to bring it from Europe. Luxuries were shipped, at incredible cost, across the Atlantic and then up the Amazon river for many miles. Some people sent their laundry all the way back to Paris to be washed and ironed. But the rubber tappers themselves, the *seringeiros,* lived in terrible conditions in remote parts of the forests, working like slaves. Few of them made their fortunes.

Suddenly, in the 1920s, the boom ended. Rubber seeds from the Amazon had been taken to the Far East, especially to Malaya, to be grown on plantations. These were very successful, and the rubber was easier and cheaper to collect than from the wild Amazon rubber trees, scattered all over the rain forest. The huge supply of rubber from the Far East brought the world price down. Although several attempts to cultivate rubber plantations in the Amazon basin were made, they failed because of disease and poor soil conditions.

Since the arrival of Europeans, trade and industry has mostly been based on taking natural resources out of the Amazon basin to be used elsewhere. Today valuable hardwoods are cut down in

Above A ferry on the Madeira River is loaded with bricks to be taken upstream.

Below *Ouro* means gold: in the towns many shops buy gold from the *garimpeiros*.

the forest and exported abroad. But forestry has never become a major industry. Profitable hardwood trees are hard to locate, and when found they are not easy to take out of the forests.

But gold is found in many parts of the Amazon basin. There are possibly a million men (called *garimpeiros*) in the Amazon region now, searching for gold. When word gets around that gold has been found, a "gold rush" starts and the *garimpeiros* move into a new area. Some of them dig for gold and others pan out gravel and mud from streams and rivers, but many have big dredgers on the rivers, which can quickly dig and sift through huge amounts of mud, sand, and rocks on the riverbed.

A boat from Rio de Janeiro, thousands of miles away, waits to load up at the floating dock in Manaus.

Industrial projects

The largest industrial projects in the Amazon basin are either for mining or hydroelectric power. The biggest development is at Carajás, where huge deposits of iron ore and other minerals have been found. In the forests of Peru, Ecuador, and Bolivia, companies are drilling for oil and gas and piping it up over the Andes. The Amazon also has great possibilities for the provision of cheap energy for poor countries like Brazil. Two huge dams have been built, at Tucurui and Balbina, to supply electricity to industry and to cities in Brazil. Several more dams are planned on the Tocantins and Xingu rivers.

There is some manufacturing industry within the Amazon basin, based in the cities where transportation is good, such as at Belém, with its new fast highway to the markets of southern Brazil. The other big industrial area is at Manaus. Here there has been a boom of new industries since the Brazilian government set up a tax-free zone to encourage business and industry.

Oil storage tanks at Porto Velho. Tankers carry the oil to remote villages.

Waterways, highways, and planes

As transportation in the Amazon basin changes, so do the opportunities for trade. The Amazon River has always been the main highway and is still vital for transportation to most of the people who live there. There are thousands of miles of navigable waterways throughout the basin. One reason that cities far up the Amazon have managed to be successful at all is because ocean-going ships can sail 2,486 miles inland from the Atlantic Ocean.

The biggest changes in the region have been the building of roads like the Trans-Amazonian Highway. This road is not as grand as it sounds; rains often wash the 3,107-mile road away and it becomes impassable. There are no bridges on the Amazon River itself, nor on many of its tributaries, and so vehicles have to be taken across by ferry Some new roads have been surfaced and built to last, like the Belém to Brasilia Highway. Building roads is helping the growth of industry in the region because transporting goods by road is a much faster way of moving them than by river boat. The roads have also encouraged people to settle in new parts of the region.

Airplanes too, have opened up the Amazon: Manaus has an international airport, and a flight to Miami takes just a few hours. Small airplanes are used to reach towns and villages tucked away deep in the forest, which would otherwise take many weeks to reach by boat and car.

The Tucurui Dam

The building of this dam was begun in 1975. It is the largest hydroelectric project in the world. Once they are working, dams like this can provide plenty of cheap electricity. But billions of dollars were spent building the dam, and 965 sq. miles of rain forest had to be flooded. Eight thousand people lost their homes, including many Amazon Indians. Thousands of animals died as the valley was flooded. Much of the electricity goes to big power industrial projects and is of little help to ordinary people, especially those who live in the area. The dam itself may run into problems. Rotting trees and plants in the reservoir have caused the water to become very acid, and this may damage the turbines. There is also a real concern that the reservoir may become choked with weeds. Malaria has increased because mosquitoes breed in the still water of the reservoir.

Most roads are just dirt tracks. They are often washed away in the rainy season.

6

Towns and Cities of the Amazon

Manaus is situated in the middle of the Amazon basin. It lies on the Rio Negro, just upstream from where this river joins the Amazon. The city's population is more than one million. There are shops, office buildings, and hotels, surrounded by suburbs, slums, and industrial complexes, sprawling to the edge of the rain forest. As well as its international airport, Manaus has a road link north to Venezuela, and another road leads south to Bolivia, which is unusable in the wet season.

During the rubber boom, Manaus grew from a tiny settlement to be the richest city in the Americas, even

Many famous opera and ballet stars performed at the Manaus Opera House, which was built at the height of the rubber boom. The ironwork was shipped from Scotland and the stone from Italy.

A shopping street in Manaus. People come from all over Brazil to set up business and to buy goods there.

though the only contact with the outside world was by boat. Electric streetcars ran along the roads, there was a fashionable nightlife, and international stars sang at its opera house. In order to make loading rubber on to ships easier, a special floating dock was built to cope with changes in river levels of up to 51 feet. However, after the rubber boom ended in the 1920s, the city rapidly became a jungle backwater again.

In 1967 the Brazilian government made Manaus a free-trade zone, where companies setting up business did not have to pay taxes. This encouraged new industries and the population of the city grew fast. Japanese electronics companies moved to the new industrial complexes, employing local people to assemble computers, calculators, and other products. Today Brazilians come to Manaus to buy cheap electrical goods, and foreign tourists and scientists fly there to visit the Amazon rain forest.

Near the mouth of the Amazon, only 90 miles from the sea, lies Belém. It is a bustling modern city but with many old buildings as reminders of the prosperous days of the rubber boom. In the seventeenth century, Belém became a center for cocoa, spices, and the slave trade. Today it is an important port and industrial center, with a population of more than a million. Brazil nuts and timber are two of the rain forest products shipped out from Belém. Unlike other Amazon towns, it has good road connections with the outside world.

The people in Belém are some of the most varied in the Amazon region. Not only are most a mixture of native American people and Portuguese; many also have African blood. Millions of African slaves were brought in to work on sugarcane plantations on the coast when Brazil was first settled by the Portuguese in the sixteenth century.

Many Japanese came to start a new

life in Brazil in the 1930s. They have set up successful farms in the area. However, like Manaus, Belém has thousands of poor people who have come to the city looking for work; many are homeless or live in riverside slums on the edge of the city.

Far up the river, nearly 2,485 miles from the sea, lies Iquitos, the main town of the Upper Amazon. It is completely cut off except by air or boat. This is the farthest up the Amazon that ocean-going ships can dock. Iquitos grew, like the other cities, during the rubber boom. Recently it has become a center for oil exploration in the Peruvian forests and

Left A boy sells pineapples and cacao pods (in the baskets) from a waterfront stall in Belém.

its population has grown to 350,000. It is one of the wettest cities in the Amazon basin, with heavy rain falling nearly every day of the year. Homes in the huge slum area by the river are built high on stilts to avoid the frequent floods.

Lying by the Rio Madeira, in the region called Rondônia, is Porto Velho. Over the last twenty years it has changed from a small town to a modern city of 450,000 people. Porto Velho has grown because thousands of settlers have moved to the region. There has been a gold rush in Rondônia, and several agricultural development projects have been set up in the area. A good road connects Porto Velho to the rest of Brazil, which has improved traveling and transporting goods.

Boats are used for getting to and from floating homes and waterfront houses in Iquitos.

33

7
Living by the Amazon

Life near the source of the Amazon is very different from that elsewhere on the river. The high Andes mountains are cold and bleak so that it is difficult to grow much more than corn, potatoes, and a few other vegetables. Many of the people there are Andean Indians, descended from the Incas. On the slopes of the Andes mountains they raise herds of llamas for their wool, in much the same way as their ancestors have done for centuries.

These *Caboclos* live in a clearing beside the Madeira River. They grow bananas which are taken by passing boats to the nearest town for sale.

Luciano, a *Caboclos* schoolboy

"My name is Luciano and here I am, with my friends, digging up mandioca which has been planted by my father. Some people call it manioc or cassava. It is a root vegetable that can be ground up into flour and made into bread. Everyone here eats it. This is sweet mandioca which I like very much. But there is also a bitter mandioca. The bitter kind has to be carefully washed and poisonous juice squeezed out of it before it can be cooked."

The *Caboclos*

In the tropical Amazon basin, many people outside the towns and cities live very simple lives, quite similar to the lives of the native peoples of the Amazon. These people are known as *Caboclos* and they are of mixed race—European (mainly Portuguese or Spanish) and Indian. They grow manioc (an edible root) and bananas, and catch fish.

Crops cannot be grown for long on the same patch of poor Amazon soil because it has so few nutrients. So after a few years, farmers have to clear new land for their crops. Some people make a little extra money from gathering Brazil nuts, fruit, or rubber. On Marajó Island, farmers raise water buffalo for meat and hides.

Most *Caboclos* live by a river because it provides water for drinking and washing, and fish to eat. Some depend on the regular flooding of the *varzea* to bring the rich sediment that fertilizes the land.

The *Caboclos'* rivers are their roads too, and children learn from a very young age how to paddle a canoe. In the flood season the large rivers can be dangerous because whole tree trunks sweep downriver and riverbanks sometimes crumble into the water.

Houses are simple, usually built with plain wooden planks and roofed with a thatch made from palm leaves or with sheets of corrugated metal. Sometimes they are built on stilts and raised above the ground, which keeps them dry in heavy rain and floods.

It is a very isolated life for many people living in the Amazon basin, and there is often no school nearby for the children. The nearest hospital is likely to be many hours away by boat. Health is often a serious problem: many dangerous diseases, such as cholera and tuberculosis, are still found there. Perhaps because so many children die young, families are large—often ten and sometimes as many as twenty children in one family.

Floating houses rise and fall with the changing level of the river.

Land clearance

Many settlers from poorer areas have come to the Amazon basin in recent years, hoping to start a new life there. Unlike the *Caboclos*, they usually settle beside the new roads. Here they clear a patch of land, try to grow food, and plant a cash crop such as coffee. In Rondônia in Brazil, the population tripled between 1970 and 1980, as new settlers arrived.

Settlers clear forest land to grow crops.

It is difficult to enforce the law in these remote areas: if someone wants a piece of land they take it. Like the Wild West, people hire gunmen and there are sometimes killings.

Cattle ranching is now the biggest use of land in the Amazon. For several years the Brazilian government encouraged companies to clear land for grazing. The government promised that companies that cleared the land would not be taxed, so land clearance became popular and profitable. Vast areas of forest were slashed and burned down. It was said that the cleared land would make good pasture, but it becomes almost useless because the soil is so infertile. The pasture dies and is taken over by weeds. To keep good pasture for cattle requires huge amounts of chemical fertilizers. Often it is simpler just to abandon the land and clear a new area. This is usually done by burning the forests, because this is easier than cutting down the trees. Every year, in the dry season, smoke from the *queimada,* the burnings, fills the Amazon's skies.

Above A tiny settlement lies beside a new road running through the Amazon rain forest.

Below These zebu cattle were introduced from Asia. They do well in the Amazonian climate.

37

8

The Amazon Indians–A Vanishing Race

Mario, Amazon Indian

"My Brazilian name is Mario, although I am an Indian. I live in the city of Porto Velho and I'm working to help my people. We've made these posters because we are going to hold a special Indian week in the Amazon, to demonstrate our traditions and culture. We also want to make people aware of what is happening to the Indians in Brazil. Few seem to care what happens to us. They just come here and chop down the trees, and then we have nowhere to grow our food or to hunt. We have lived here for thousands of years and it's our land."

Nobody has learned how to live in the Amazon better than its native peoples. For thousands of years the rivers and forests have provided them with every-

An Amazon Indian demonstrates how his forest medicines can put animals such as this snake to sleep.

thing they needed. Because they have lived in harmony with nature, they have not damaged the rivers and the forests.

During the last 400 years, the way of life of the Amazon Indians has been almost totally destroyed. It is believed that there were about five million of them living in the Amazon basin before the arrival of the Europeans. Now there are fewer than 200,000. Although many died fighting the Europeans or as slaves, by far the biggest killers were diseases, which the settlers brought with them. Even a mild illness like influenza could kill because the Amazon Indians had no natural resistance to it. Smallpox, measles, plague, and dysentery are diseases that have wiped out many thousands of people.

Xingu people living in the Xingu River region rethatch a house using palm fronds.

The few remaining Amazon Indians who keep their traditional way of life live deep in the rain forest. They grow crops like manioc, bananas, corn, and tobacco. They move on every few years, to clear a fresh patch of land in the forest. The area they clear is small and the forest is able to grow back again after a few years. The river is vitally important because it provides fish to eat. Since they only take what they need to survive and do not over-fish the rivers, they always have plenty of food and do not damage the environment.

Some Amazon Indians hunt animals like the tapir or wild pig for food, or they may kill birds for their feathers to use as decoration. They hunt using darts and blowpipes, or bows and arrows. The darts or arrows are often tipped with poison from rain forest plants. The trees and plants of the forest not only provide food like berries, nuts, honey, and spices, but also rope made from lianas and other plants to make hammocks and baskets. The Indians also know which forest trees and plants are good for medicines and drugs.

Indians bring bananas to market by boat.

Different tribes of Amazon Indians have different customs. In the northwest Amazon region, many have houses called *malocas,* where the whole tribe lives together, sometimes as many as two hundred people. Usually the *malocas* are made of wood and palm thatch, with a whole in the roof to let out smoke. Each family has a corner of the building for their hammocks and other possessions. Few Indians wear clothes, but instead they decorate their bodies with paint and wear colorful jewelery made from beads and feathers.

Traditionally, the Amazon Indians believe every living thing has a spirit—perhaps a person, a tree, a jaguar, or a piranha. Priests called shamans are in touch with the spirits, and if someone is in trouble, the shaman will try to contact the bad spirit who is causing the problem and chase it away. Ceremonies and festivals are important in the Indians' lives and are celebrated with music and dancing. Flutes, drums, and maracas are made with wood, bones, nutshells, and skins.

For many Amazon Indians, life is no longer like this. Because of land clearance, many have lost their forest homes and their traditional customs and culture. Some have settled in permanent homes, wear clothes, and have been converted to Christianity.

A few tribes now live in special reserves, set up by the governments of Brazil and other Amazon countries. Here, the Indians can continue their traditional ways; but their problems do not cease. Their lands are invaded by *garimpeiros* and others, who attack the Indians and introduce diseases. The governments themselves have taken their lands for road building and mining projects.

The Amazon Indians have no control over what happens to them as they have no say in the government of their countries. But people from around the world are now trying to draw attention to the plight of the Indians.

A cleared patch of land is sown with manioc by native Indians.

40

9
The Amazon Under Threat

Although settlers have been coming to the Amazon region for centuries, it is only recently that people have started to over-use the Amazon's resources and force unnatural changes on the environment. The Amazon's water cycle, and the constant replenishment of nutrients for the plants and animals of the rain forest, are all part of a carefully balanced system. It takes very little to upset this and cause harmful changes which cannot be reversed.

Building roads through the rain forest destroys trees and causes soil erosion.

Heavy machinery is trucked in to clear more land, and an oil pipeline carries oil from Ecuador across the rain forest toward the coast.

Destruction of the rain forest

Cattle ranching has probably had more long-term effects than anything else in the Amazon because of the size of the areas that have been cleared for pasture. The fact that it does not make good pasture in the long-term does not stop the forest destruction because people see that they can still make some money in the short-term. Mining and all the industrial development that goes with it, like the huge Carajás Project, also clears vast areas of forest. Indian tribes have to be relocated. The same happens when the forest is flooded for dams, as has occurred at Tucurui.

Road building is changing the face of the Amazon. Many trees are felled as the bulldozers carve a route through the forest. New roads block streams, and the water collects in lakes so that the trees become waterlogged and die. Roads also make it easier for valuable hardwood trees to be reached; unfortunately, in order to cut down one hardwood tree

The Carajás Iron Ore Project
This massive project, to exploit the world's largest deposit of iron ore, cost more than 62 billion dollars. It covers a vast area of what was once rain forest. The main development is the huge iron ore mine, and there are housing developments and industrial buildings all around. Charcoal, made from wood, has been the main source of fuel for processing the ore, and will mean the felling of all the forests in the area. A railroad link to a new port was built straight through an Indian reserve. Shanty towns are growing quickly all over the Carajás area.

many other trees have to be felled to reach it.

The roads pave a way for new settlers, who build new towns and farms. Many find their land is poor and they are unable to grow enough food to eat, let alone raise a cash crop to bring them some money. If they can, they clear new land for their crops. The traditional way the Indians and *Caboclos* live, clearing small patches of forest, works well as ong as there are not too many people. If there are too many, the forest cannot heal itself properly. It does not have time to grow back and build up the nutrients again.

Every minute of every day in the Amazon basin an area of forest the size of fourteen football fields disappears. In 1987, an area almost twice the size of Pennsylvania was destroyed. Once a large patch has been cleared, the forest is unlikely to grow back again. There are no trees nearby to provide new seeds and, without the forest cover, the nutrients will soon be washed out of the soil. Heavy rain may erode the soil away altogether. What is then left is a wasteland, overgrown with weeds, and in some places just a desert.

Cleared land soon loses its fertility and becomes a wasteland.

Heavy rains can wash away soil that has no tree cover, or may cause landslides.

There are no tree roots left to trap
rainwater, and it runs off the land. This
can sometimes cause floods because soil
that is washed away may block rivers.
Clearing such large areas of forest may
change the climate too. More than half
the rain falling in the Amazon basin
comes from transpiration by the trees—
so if they disappear, there will be less
rainfall. It is not certain what the long-
term result of destroying rain forests
will be. It is known that rain forests
have an effect on weather worldwide, so
their destruction may possibly affect us
all in the future.

There are other results from the development of the Amazon region. Nearly
half the world's species of animals,
birds, fish, and plants are found there.
Several of these are under threat of
extinction because of forest clearance
and from the trade in rare plants and
animals and wild birds.

Rivers, like the Tapajós, are becoming
polluted with mercury, which is used in
the process of obtaining gold. Near the
big cities, rivers are also becoming polluted with industrial and other wastes.

New roads block streams which then form
lakes so that trees growing in the soil become
waterlogged and die.

The need for wise use of resources

Many of the countries of the Amazon basin are very poor, with terrible economic
and social problems. To them the huge
amount of land, the minerals, the possibilities for hydroelectricity, the animals
and plants, are resources which they
want to use, just as developed countries
have done in the past.

For example, Brazil owes billions of
dollars to foreign banks and sees projects like the Carajás Project as a means
to earn money to repay their debt.
Encouraging the poor to come and settle
on new land in the Amazon basin
seemed a way of helping them. People in
these countries do not worry about the

Life goes on quietly for this family of *Caboclos*, living deep in the heart of the rain forest, beside the river that provides them with all they need.

problems of a hundred thousand Amazon Indians, when their populations of millions have barely enough to eat. However, even while using the resources of the Amazon, the poor still remain poor, and the economic situation in these countries does not improve.

Although people are learning about the effects that development in the Amazon basin is causing, many still see the area as a resource to be used until everything in it runs out or disappears.

Plundering the Amazon rain forest may help a few people in the short-term, but in the long-term we may see the destruction of the whole area.

Studies are being carried out to try to find solutions to use the resources of the Amazon in ways that are not so harmful and irreversible. Perhaps we should learn from the traditional methods of farming and harvesting the forests, which have worked so well for thousands of years.

Glossary

Ancestors People in the family who are no longer alive, such as great-grandparents and their parents and grandparents.

Caboclos The Portuguese name for poor people of mixed race—European and Indian—who live outside the towns and cities of the Amazon basin.

Cash crop Something that is grown to sell rather than for the family to eat.

Catchment area An area of land from which a river or river basin receives its water.

Continent A large land mass.

Convert To cause someone to change their ideas or beliefs.

Descendants Relatives of animals or people who lived long ago.

Dredgers Special ships that are used for digging up mud from the bottom of rivers or harbors.

Erode To wear away land by the action of water.

Evolved To have developed gradually.

Exploiting Making use of natural resources.

Extinction When animals or plants have died out and none are left.

Fertile Land that is full of nutrients and can produce good crops.

Grazing Vegetation that is grown for animals to eat.

Harmony When everything works well together.

Hydroelectric power Power produced by the pressure of falling water.

Incas South American Indian people, whose great empire in the Andes lasted from about 1100 to 1600 A.D.

Influenza An illness commonly known as the "flu."

Jesuit A Christian (Roman Catholic) missionary. Many of them traveled to remote parts of the Amazon region to try to convert the native peoples.

Lianas Woody climbing plants.

Llamas Animals living in the Andes, related to the camel. They are used for carrying things, and for their wool and meat.

Malaria An illness caused by the bite of a certain kind of mosquito that lives in hot, swampy areas.

Manioc A widely cultivated plant in tropical countries, also called cassava. It is an important source of food.

Maracas Musical instruments that are shaken to make a rattling sound.

Mercury A liquid metal.

Natural resources Natural products that we can use.

Navigable Describes a waterway that is wide, deep, and safe enough for boats.

Nutrients Food that plants (or animals) need to help them grow.

Pan To wash gravel in a pan to separate out valuable minerals.

Pasture Vegetation, where animals are brought to graze.

Plantations Estates where cash crops are grown on a large scale.

Recycled Used again.

Reserves Areas of land set aside for a special purpose, such as a home for Indians to live on or for rare plants and animals.

Resistance The ability to fight disease.

Rodent A gnawing animal such as a rat, mouse, squirrel, or porcupine.

Silt Fine mud or clay carried by a river.

Species A group of animals or plants that are similar.

Transpire To lose water into the air, in the form of water vapor, especially from a plant's leaves.

Turbines Engines powered by falling water, steam, or gas, that turn wheels to produce electricity.

Water cycle Circulation of the Earth's water, in which water evaporates from the sea into the atmosphere, where it falls as rain or snow, returning to the sea through rivers.

BOOKS TO READ AND USEFUL ADDRESSES

Books to Read

Ashford, Moyra. *Brazil.* Steck-Vaughn, 1991.

Banks, Martin. *Conserving Rain Forests.* Raintree Steck-Vaughn, 1990.

Haverstock, Nathan A. *Brazil in Pictures.* Lerner, 1987.

Lewington, Anna. *Rain Forest Amerindians.* Raintree Steck-Vaughn, 1992.

Morrison, Marion. *Ecuador, Peru, and Bolivia.* Raintree Steck-Vaughn, 1992.

Roland-Entwistle, Theodore. *Jungles and Rainforests.* Silver Burdett Press, 1987.

Useful Addresses

Conservation Foundation
1250 24th St., N.W., Suite 500
Washington, DC 20037

The Environment Defense Fund
Dept. P, 257 Park Ave. South
New York, NY 10010

Friends of the Earth
1045 Sansome Street
San Francisco, CA 94111

Friends of the Earth Foundation
530 Seventh Street, S.E.
Washington, DC 20003

Greenpeace
1611 Connecticut Avenue, N.W.
Washington, DC 20009

Picture acknowledgments

All photographs are by Julia Waterlow except the following: ©Craig Duncan/DDB Stock Photo cover; Omar Barugue 9; Sue Cunningham 39, 40 (lower); Mary Evans 19, 20 (top); Eye Ubiquitous 36 (lower); Tony Morrison/South American Pictures 6, 20 (lower), 23 (top), 28, 33; Edward Parker 41, 42, 44 (top). The map on page 5 is by Peter Bull Design. Artwork on pages 7, 9, 12 and 14 is by John Yates.

INDEX

Numbers in **bold** refer to illustrations